OUR SOLAR SYSTEM
THE SUN

by Philip Wolny

BrightPoint Press

San Diego, CA

© 2023 BrightPoint Press
an imprint of ReferencePoint Press, Inc.
Printed in the United States

For more information, contact:
BrightPoint Press
PO Box 27779
San Diego, CA 92198
www.BrightPointPress.com

ALL RIGHTS RESERVED.

No part of this work covered by the copyright hereon may be reproduced or used in any form or by any means—graphic, electronic, or mechanical, including photocopying, recording, taping, web distribution, or information storage retrieval systems—without the written permission of the publisher.

LIBRARY OF CONGRESS CATALOGING-IN-PUBLICATION DATA

Names: Wolny, Philip, author.
Title: The sun / by Philip Wolny.
Description: San Diego, CA: BrightPoint Press, [2023] | Series: Our solar system | Includes bibliographical references and index. | Audience: Grades 10-12
Identifiers: LCCN 2022003710 (print) | LCCN 2022003711 (eBook) | ISBN 9781678204105 (hardcover) | ISBN 9781678204112 (eBook)
Subjects: LCSH: Sun.
Classification: LCC QB521 .W65 2023 (print) | LCC QB521 (eBook) | DDC 523.7--dc23/eng20220318
LC record available at https://lccn.loc.gov/2022003710
LC eBook record available at https://lccn.loc.gov/2022003711

CONTENTS

AT A GLANCE	4
INTRODUCTION JOURNEY TO THE CENTER OF THE SOLAR SYSTEM	6
CHAPTER ONE HOW DOES THE SUN WORK?	12
CHAPTER TWO THE SUN'S LIFE CYCLE	26
CHAPTER THREE THE STORY OF SOLAR DISCOVERY	36
CHAPTER FOUR OBSERVING THE SUN TODAY	44
Glossary	58
Source Notes	59
For Further Research	60
Index	62
Image Credits	63
About the Author	64

AT A GLANCE

- The Sun is a star. It is the closest star to Earth, and it is the center of the solar system.

- The Sun makes up most of the matter in the solar system. Compared to Earth and the other planets, the Sun is gigantic.

- The Sun is mostly made of gas. Most of that gas is in the form of super-hot plasma.

- The Sun acts like a huge nuclear reactor. Inside it, hydrogen turns into helium. This process creates light and heat.

- The Sun was born about 4.6 billion years ago. It started as a nebula and later became a protostar.

- The Sun will expand into a red giant billions of years in the future. It will eventually use up all its hydrogen fuel and die out over many more billions of years.

- The Sun was considered a god by many early civilizations. Early scientists believed it went around the Earth. Later theories and discoveries showed that Earth and the other planets orbit the Sun.

- Telescopes have helped humans observe and study the Sun in more detail for the last few hundred years.

- Satellites and solar probes have been launched to study the Sun. The Parker Solar Probe, launched in 2018, is designed to get closer than ever before.

INTRODUCTION

JOURNEY TO THE CENTER OF THE SOLAR SYSTEM

It's before dawn on August 12, 2018, in Florida. Spotlights illuminate a huge orange-and-white rocket on a launchpad. On the top of the rocket is a car-size spacecraft. It is the Parker Solar Probe (PSP). The probe is being launched by the National Aeronautics and Space

Administration (NASA). This is the US national space agency. The PSP's goal is to learn more about the Sun. It will fly closer to the Sun than any mission has before.

The countdown reaches zero. Flames from the rocket light up the darkness. The

The Parker Solar Probe blasted off atop a Delta IV Heavy rocket.

rocket lifts off the pad. It zooms into the dark sky. A few minutes later, it is in space.

For several years, the PSP flies through the solar system. Finally, it approaches the Sun. The closer it gets, the faster the probe goes. It reaches a top speed of 430,000 miles per hour (700,000 km/h). The side of the spacecraft facing the Sun heats up to 2,500°F (1,380°C). A heat shield protects the equipment inside.

Earth is about 93 million miles (150 million km) from the Sun. The PSP gets as close as 3.8 million miles (6 million km). It studies the Sun's magnetic fields. It looks at the

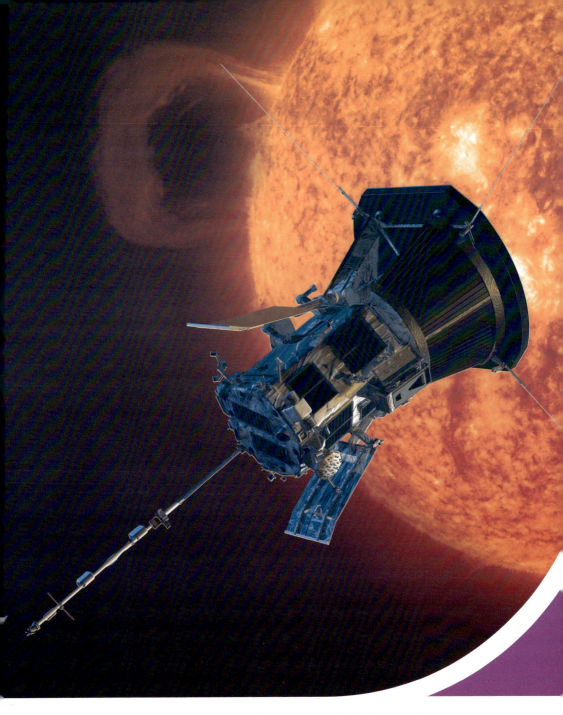

The Parker Solar Probe is designed to keep the heat shield pointed in exactly the right direction to protect the spacecraft.

particles the Sun gives off. It takes pictures. All of this data will help scientists learn more about the Sun, the closest star to Earth.

OUR LOCAL STAR

Without the Sun, life as we know it would be impossible. It provides heat and light to Earth. Its heat keeps Earth at a livable temperature. Its energy helps plants grow.

The Sun is at the center of our solar system. Earth and the other planets move around it in paths known as orbits. So do asteroids, comets, and other space objects. The shapes of these orbits are round,

The Sun is crucial to life on Earth.

but they are not perfect circles. They are oval-shaped.

The Sun is the biggest and brightest object in Earth's sky. Humans have studied the Sun throughout history. This is a continuing journey of discovery. Today, tools such as the PSP teach us even more.

1
HOW DOES THE SUN WORK?

The Sun is a star. Stars are mostly made of gas. They are often huge compared to planets. The gases that make up stars go through processes that give off large amounts of energy. This energy comes in the form of light and heat.

People can see thousands of stars on a clear night. These look like tiny points of light. This is because they are very distant. The Sun looks far bigger. It is much closer to Earth than other stars. The Sun is 93 million miles (150 million km) from Earth. The next nearest star is about 25 trillion miles (40 trillion km) from Earth. That's about 270,000 times farther away.

The Sun is a star, just like the many stars that can be seen on a dark, clear night.

THE SUN'S SIZE

The Sun is considered a medium-size star. Compared to Earth, though, it is huge. Science writer C. Alex Young writes, "It is difficult to get a true feel for how big it is because nothing in our daily life comes even close. . . . If you think of the Sun as a basketball, the Earth would only be the size of the head of a pin."[1]

The Sun is about 864,400 miles (1,391,000 km) across. This is about 109 times Earth's diameter. The Sun could fit about 1.3 million Earths inside. Its mass is around 330,000 times as much as Earth.

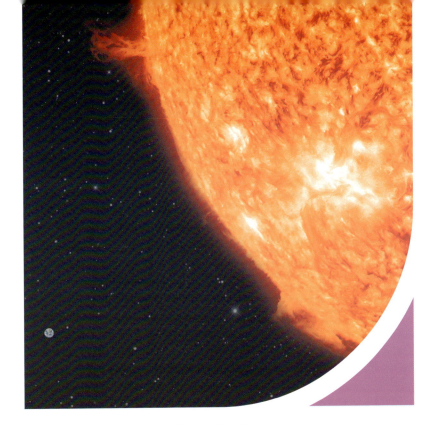

The Sun is far larger than Earth.

The Sun is by far the largest object in the solar system. It contains 99.86 percent of the solar system's total matter.

A BIG BALL OF ENERGY

Some planets, like Earth, are mostly solid. Stars are different. They are mostly made of gas. Heat and pressure turn the gas into a form called **plasma**.

The Sun contains several different layers, or zones. The center is known as the **core**. It makes up only 2 percent of the Sun's volume. It is extremely dense. As a result, the core makes up almost half of the Sun's mass.

Inside the core, hydrogen atoms are pushed so tightly together that they combine into helium atoms. This process is called **nuclear fusion**. It releases huge amounts of energy. Every second, the Sun changes nearly 700 million tons (635 million

The Sun's process of nuclear fusion releases amazing amounts of energy.

metric tons) of hydrogen into helium. The energy released creates incredible heat. The core can reach 27 million°F (15 million°C).

Above the core lies the radiative zone. Energy released in the core enters the radiative zone as light. Light can bounce

Studying the Sun with different instruments reveals different features, helping scientists learn more about its structure.

around in this zone for hundreds of thousands of years before leaving the Sun. The heat and light eventually travel outward toward the surface.

Past the radiative zone is a cooler area. It is called the convection zone. It makes up 30 percent of the Sun's volume. Hot gases move outward. Cooler material goes inward. The outer part of this zone marks the surface of the Sun. It is the deepest part humans can see with scientific instruments.

ABOVE THE SUN'S SURFACE

The next layer, the photosphere, rests on top of the convection zone. The temperature here is about 9,980°F (5,530°C). This zone releases the light humans can see. It is about 250 miles

THE SUN'S LAYERS

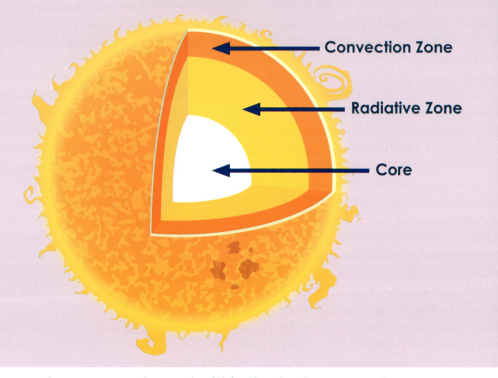

The energy released within the Sun's core makes its way outward through the Sun's layers before emerging and traveling out into the solar system.

(400 km) thick. The photosphere is where sunspots occur.

Above the photosphere lies a region called the chromosphere. The chromosphere reaches as high as 1,300 miles (2,100 km) above the Sun's surface. At the top of this zone, temperatures rise higher. They can reach up to 14,000°F (7,700°C).

The top of the chromosphere marks the transition region. Here, the temperature skyrockets even more. It rises to more than 900,000°F (500,000°C). Past the transition region is the outermost layer, called the corona.

The corona starts at about 1,300 miles (2,100 km) above the surface. Temperatures here can rise to about 2 million°F (1.1 million°C). People can safely look at the Sun using a special telescope called a coronagraph.

SOLAR PHENOMENA

The Sun is an active object. Scientists observe many things happening on its surface. These are known as solar phenomena. One example is solar

PLASMA

The hot form of gas that makes up much of the Sun is called plasma. It is a fourth state of matter, along with liquids, solids, and gases. It has far more energy than the other states. Plasma is the most common type of material in the universe. On Earth, it can be seen in neon signs.

flares. Solar flares are large explosions of electromagnetic energy from the surface. This energy is stored in the corona. The large amount of energy released can travel far. Flares can even disrupt radio signals on Earth.

Sunspots are dark areas on the Sun's surface. They appear because of the star's magnetic activity. Sunspots move across the Sun. They are cooler than the areas around them. Sunspots can be many thousands of miles across. Scientists observe an increase in sunspot activity about every eleven years.

Another solar event is a coronal mass ejection (CME). CMEs occur when the Sun releases large amounts of plasma and parts of its magnetic field. These eruptions near the Sun's surface can release as much power as 20 million nuclear weapons. They can travel at 1 million miles per hour (1.6 million km/h). Most never hit Earth. Sometimes they do, however. Direct hits can badly damage satellites. They can even disrupt electrical systems.

A constant stream of particles from the Sun travels through space. It is known as the solar wind. The particles hit atoms in

Coronal mass ejections release huge amounts of energy into space.

Earth's atmosphere. This causes light to be released, creating an **aurora**. Aurorae are easiest to see in the extreme north and south. When CMEs hit Earth, they can cause these aurorae to flare up. Aurorae can then be seen from much more of the planet than usual.

2
THE SUN'S LIFE CYCLE

Billions of years ago, the Sun did not exist. Instead, in its place there was a huge cloud of gas and dust. A cloud like this is known as a **nebula**. About 4.6 billion years ago, things started to change. The solar nebula would become the Sun we know today.

Nebulae are the beginning stages of solar systems. They are sometimes known as star nurseries. Some nebulae grow bigger and denser. Gravity attracts more gas and dust together. The more material comes together, the stronger the gravity becomes.

New stars are born in vast clouds of gas and dust.

A PROTOSTAR IS BORN

The Sun was born when gravity brought huge amounts of dust and gas together. As its gravity increased, this cloud of material collapsed on itself. More material was pulled toward its center.

The collapsing nebula spun faster and faster. Much of the material formed into a ball at the center. This ball was a protostar. The rest orbited this protostar in a disk shape. Most of the material later became the Sun. Some of it formed the solar system's other objects, including Earth. The process took around 100 million years.

When enough material swirls together, a protostar can form.

Science writer Nola Taylor Tillman points out that 100 million years is "an eye-blink in astronomical terms."[2] The protostar grew. It became hotter and denser.

HERE COMES THE SUN

Eventually, this density and heat started the process of nuclear fusion. The Sun became what is known as a main sequence star. It is still in this state today. About 90 percent of stars are main sequence stars. This means that they fuse hydrogen to make helium.

The Sun's size helped decide its fate. Bigger stars burn through their hydrogen much more quickly. A star ten times bigger than the Sun may last only about 20 million years. The Sun has been burning for billions of years.

The Sun's gravity creates tremendous force that pulls its matter inward. The fusion process gives off so much energy it pushes the star outward. The balance of these two forces helps keep the Sun stable. This also keeps the Sun about the same size for this part of its life cycle.

THE SUN IN MIDDLE AGE

The Sun is about 4.6 billion years old. It is about halfway through its life cycle. It continues to use up its hydrogen. Scientists predict this part of the star's life will end when the Sun is about 10 billion years old.

STAR SIZES

A star's size affects how it looks. Larger stars are hotter and bluer in color. Smaller ones are cooler and redder. The Sun lies about halfway between these two extremes. It is a medium-size star that is white in color.

As its fuel runs out, the core of the Sun will shrink. It will also get hotter. The pressure in its core will increase. This will speed up the fusion process.

The amount of light the Sun emits is increasing. In about 1.1 billion years, the Sun will be about 10 percent brighter. By about 3.5 billion years from now, it will be 40 percent brighter. The Sun's heat will boil away Earth's oceans. The water in Earth's atmosphere will disappear. This includes the ice caps. It will be too hot for any plants or animals to survive. Earth's atmosphere will be hot and dry.

Scientists believe that in the distant future, the Sun will be brighter and hotter, causing Earth's oceans to dry up.

THE FINAL STAGES OF THE SUN

In about 5.4 billion years, the Sun's hydrogen will finally run out. The helium in the core will become unstable and collapse inward. The core will get even denser and hotter. The increased heat will cause the Sun's outer layers to expand. It will become a **red giant**. The Sun will grow to swallow up Mercury and Venus. It may even extend as far as Earth.

As a red giant, the Sun will be 256 times larger than it is now. But it will be only about 67 percent of its present mass. The Sun's life as a red giant will last only about 120 million years. Eventually, the Sun will dim and cool. Its outer layers will drift away.

What's left will be a white dwarf. It will still be incredibly hot. But it will be much smaller than before. The white dwarf that used to be the Sun will have about 50 percent of its previous mass. It will be about the size of

After the Sun's red giant stage, scientists believe its outer layers will drift away into space, leaving behind a smaller, cooler star.

Earth. It will then continue to cool for many billions of years. At some point in the distant future, scientists believe it will stop giving off any light. At that point, it will be known as a black dwarf.

3
THE STORY OF SOLAR DISCOVERY

The Sun has been part of stories and legends since humans first created language. Many early religions tried to explain what the Sun was. Some of them thought it was a god. There are many Sun gods in ancient faiths.

For example, the ancient Egyptians had Ra. Ra was the most important god. This was probably because of how important the Sun was. The ancient Greeks had a Sun god named Helios. In their myths, Helios rode a chariot pulled by flying horses across

The ancient Egyptian Sun god Ra is sometimes shown as having a bird's head.

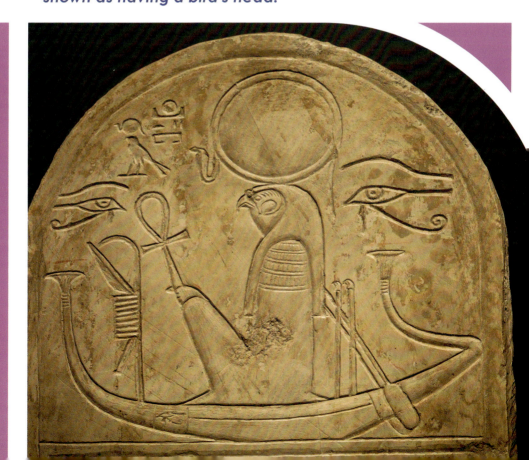

It was once thought that the other planets rotated around Earth.

the sky every day. That chariot moved the Sun. This explained why the Sun rose and moved east to west.

Astronomers are people who study space. Ancient astronomers were interested in the Sun. They tracked and measured its movements. The Greek philosopher Anaxagoras even believed the Sun was a giant, hot rock in the sky. Anaxagoras also declared, "It is the Sun that puts brightness into the Moon."[3] He was correct. The Moon's light is mostly reflected light from the Sun.

THE GEOCENTRIC MODEL

Ideas about the Sun and Earth have changed over time. Some ancient people thought the Moon, Sun, and Earth were all about the same size. Others believed the

Sun was not very far away since it looked so near. Modern people know that the Sun is huge compared to Earth. It is also much farther away than ancient peoples thought.

People once believed Earth was the center of the universe. They thought the Sun and planets went around Earth. This was known as the geocentric model of the solar system. But one early Greek scientist believed differently. Aristarchus of Samos lived in the 200s BCE. He said the Sun was the center of the solar system. Few people took this idea seriously.

Today, statues in Poland honor the work of Copernicus.

THE HELIOCENTRIC MODEL

In 1543, the Polish astronomer Nicolaus Copernicus also said Earth revolved around the Sun. "Finally, we shall place the Sun himself at the center of the universe," he wrote.[4] This idea was called the heliocentric model of the solar system. Copernicus also thought the Earth rotated each day.

The following century, the astronomer Galileo Galilei of Italy spread these ideas. Many people resisted them. Religious leaders punished Galileo. They kept him under house arrest until he died.

Galileo and others of his time used new inventions to study space. These included telescopes. Special telescopes allowed astronomers to study the Sun. Humans cannot look directly at the Sun. This can damage the eyes. It can even blind someone permanently. Scientists invented special filters. These helped make the Sun safe to look at. Scientists later developed special types of photography to study the Sun.

THE FIRST PHOTO OF A SOLAR ECLIPSE

When the Moon passes between the Sun and Earth, this is called a solar eclipse. Prussian photographer Johann Julius Friedrich Berkowski took the first image of a solar eclipse in 1851. The picture was a daguerreotype, an early type of photography. Good images of the Sun and solar events have helped advance solar science.

4
OBSERVING THE SUN TODAY

In modern times, scientists build **observatories** to study the Sun. These are large buildings on mountaintops and other good locations for watching the skies. Observatories have huge, advanced telescopes. These inventions let astronomers see features such as sunspots and solar flares better than ever before.

Scientists' ability to study the Sun has improved greatly. In the 1900s, satellites and other spacecraft made this possible. Some satellites in Earth orbit have telescopes.

Solar observatories are specially designed for studying the Sun.

WATCHING THE SUN SAFELY

One safe way to look at the Sun without risking eye damage is by using a pinhole camera. This involves punching a hole through one piece of paper. The paper is then held up to the Sun. Directing the Sun's light onto another piece of paper will create an image of the Sun that is safe to view.

Telescopes in space don't have to look through Earth's atmosphere. They can get a clearer view of the Sun.

Space probes help scientists study the Sun too. These are spacecraft that leave Earth orbit and get closer to the Sun. They observe the Sun and collect data. Space probes have also helped people learn more about the Sun's history. They have helped scientists figure out what the Sun is made of and how it affects the planets. They have also helped scientists predict what might happen to the Sun in the future.

WATCHING THE SKIES

The California Institute of Technology built the Big Bear Solar Observatory (BBSO) in 1969. It is in the middle of Big Bear Lake in California. The observatory is at an altitude of about 6,781 feet (2,067 m) above sea level. Its location on water gives solar observers clear conditions. Normally, heat released by the ground can distort an observatory's view.

BBSO has been upgraded with advanced telescopes. Its New Solar Telescope (NST) started operating in 2009. It was renamed the Goode Solar Telescope in 2017. Its high-resolution images were the sharpest and most detailed yet taken of sunspots and other solar phenomena.

The world's biggest solar telescope is the Daniel K. Inouye Solar Telescope (DKIST). It is located at the Haleakalā Observatory in Maui, Hawaii. DKIST's main

Complex machinery keeps the Daniel K. Inouye Solar Telescope operating smoothly.

mirror measures 13 feet (4 m) across. Observatory staff use it for research on the Sun's magnetic fields. They hope to answer questions about temperatures in the corona. DKIST also studies CMEs.

SOLAR SPACECRAFT

Spacecraft have expanded solar research beyond Earth's surface. Between 1965 and 1968, NASA launched the *Pioneer* spacecraft. They studied the solar wind, cosmic rays, and magnetic fields.

NASA and West Germany teamed up to launch *Helios 1* in 1974. This was followed by *Helios 2* in 1976. The *Helios* missions studied cosmic dust and cosmic rays, magnetic and electric fields, the solar wind, and other phenomena. *Helios 2* set the record for closest flyby to the Sun, at about 27 million miles (43.43 million km).

Scientists at Kennedy Space Center in Florida prepare the SOHO spacecraft for launch.

More recent missions include NASA and the European Space Agency's Solar and Heliospheric Observatory (SOHO). NASA explains that the 1995 mission aimed to "study the Sun inside out, from its internal structure, to the extensive outer atmosphere, to the solar wind that it blows across the solar system."[5] SOHO provided scientists with the first-ever images of the convection zone of the Sun. It also revealed the structure of sunspots. SOHO uses twelve different instruments to take complex measurements.

Another space mission is Japan's *Hinode* satellite. Japan launched *Hinode* in 2006 to research the corona. Even now, there is debate about why this area of the Sun is so much hotter than lower layers.

Hinode has also helped scientists explore how the Sun changes in brightness over time. Sabrina Savage is a *Hinode*

The Hinode spacecraft captured a view of Venus passing in front of the Sun in 2012.

project scientist. In 2016 she said, "The Sun is terrifying and gorgeous, and it's also the best physics laboratory in our solar system."[6]

GETTING EVER CLOSER: THE PARKER SOLAR PROBE

In 2018, NASA launched the Parker Solar Probe (PSP). It is the fastest object people have sent into space. NASA planned for the PSP to reach a distance of less than 4 million miles from the Sun. By that time it will be going more than 430,000 miles per hour (700,000 km/h).

The PSP mission has several goals. One is to examine the movement of energy and heat through the Sun's corona. Another is figuring out how magnetic fields and other factors speed up the solar wind.

Engineers spent years designing, building, and testing the Parker Solar Probe.

PSP has four major instrument systems. The Energy Particle Instruments (EPI) track solar particles shooting toward Earth. FIELDS is a set of three different devices that measure magnetic fields. The Solar Wind Electrons Alphas and Protons (SWEAP) instruments count tiny particles in the solar wind. They also track their speed,

Studying the Sun will help teach us more about our planet's neighborhood in space.

density, and temperature. There is only one camera on PSP. This is the Wide-Field Imager for Solar Probe (WISPR). It takes pictures of the corona and the regions around it.

THE JOURNEY CONTINUES

Advanced tools, such as the PSP, add new knowledge about the Sun almost daily. Studying solar phenomena helps astronauts in space. It can also help protect the important satellites around Earth.

Knowing more about the Sun gives people more knowledge about stars in general. It also helps humans better understand the universe. The Sun makes human life possible. People will continue studying it for a very long time to come.

GLOSSARY

aurora

a display of light in the sky caused by solar activity

core

the center of something, such as the superhot and dense center of the Sun

nebula

a large cloud of gas and dust, which may or may not form into a star

nuclear fusion

a process in which two or more atoms or particles are forced together to create different ones, releasing great amounts of energy

observatories

facilities that use telescopes to study objects in space

plasma

a state of matter that is like a highly energized form of gas

red giant

a very large star, usually very old in its life cycle

SOURCE NOTES

CHAPTER ONE: HOW DOES THE SUN WORK?

1. C. Alex Young, "How Big Is the Sun?" *The Sun Today*, 2022. www.thesuntoday.com.

CHAPTER TWO: THE SUN'S LIFE CYCLE

2. Nola Taylor Tillman, "How Did the Solar System Form?" *Space*, December 13, 2021. www.space.com.

CHAPTER THREE: THE STORY OF SOLAR DISCOVERY

3. Quoted in David Warmflash, "An Ancient Greek Philosopher Was Exiled for Claiming the Moon Was a Rock, Not a God," *Smithsonian Magazine*, June 20, 2019. www.smithsonianmag.com.

4. Quoted in Thomas S. Kuhn, *The Copernican Revolution*. Cambridge, MA: Harvard University Press, 1957. p. 154.

CHAPTER FOUR: OBSERVING THE SUN TODAY

5. "SOHO: The Sun, Inside Out," *NASA*, February 9, 2021. www.nasa.gov.

6. Quoted in Nola Taylor Tillman, "How Was the Sun Formed?" *Space*, June 9, 2021. www.space.com.

FOR FURTHER RESEARCH

BOOKS

Cody Crane, *The Sun*. New York: Children's Press, 2018.

Jen Green, *The Sun and Our Solar System*. North Mankato, MN: Capstone, 2018.

Walt K. Moon, *Rockets and Space Travel*. San Diego, CA: BrightPoint Press, 2023.

INTERNET SOURCES

"A Crystal Ball into Our Solar System's Future," *Phys.org*, October 13, 2021. https://phys.org.

"Layers of the Sun," *NASA*, October 10, 2012. www.nasa.gov.

"The Sun," *European Space Agency*, July 16, 2010. www.esa.int.

WEBSITES

The European Space Agency (ESA)
www.esa.int

Scientists and engineers from many European countries work together at the European Space Agency (ESA) to build spacecraft and plan missions.

The National Aeronautics and Space Administration (NASA)
www.nasa.gov

The National Aeronautics and Space Administration (NASA) is the part of the United States federal government that controls the nation's civilian space program. It also does research on space, physics, and related fields.

National Solar Observatory (NSO)
https://nso.edu

The National Solar Observatory (NSO) is a US-based public research institute. It is a leader in physics research related to the Sun.

INDEX

Anaxagoras, 39
ancient peoples, 36–40
astronauts, 57
aurorae, 25

chromosphere, 20–21
convection zone, 19, 20, 52
Copernicus, Nicolaus, 41–42
core, 16–17, 20, 32–33
corona, 21, 23, 24, 49, 52, 54, 56
coronal mass ejection (CME), 24–25, 49

Galileo, 42
geocentric model, 39–40
gods, 36–37

heliocentric model, 41–42
hydrogen, 16–17, 30, 31, 33

life cycle, 26–35

magnetic fields, 8, 23, 24, 49, 50, 54–55

NASA, 6–7, 50–51, 54
nebulae, 26–28
nuclear fusion, 16, 29–30, 32

observatories, 44–49

Parker Solar Probe (PSP), 6–10, 54–57
photosphere, 19–20
pinhole cameras, 46
plants, 10, 32
plasma, 16, 22, 24
probes, 6–10, 46–47, 50–56

radiative zone, 17–19, 20
red giant, 34

solar flares, 22–23, 45
solar wind, 24, 50–51, 54–55
stars, 10, 12–13, 14, 27
Sun layers, 16–22
Sun's size, 14–15
sunspots, 20, 23, 45, 48, 52

white dwarf, 34

IMAGE CREDITS

Cover: © Square Motion/Shutterstock Images
5: © Sergey Nivens/Shutterstock Images
7: Bill Ingalls/HQ/NASA
9: Steve Gribben/Johns Hopkins APL/NASA
11: © Yanikap/Shutterstock Images
13: © Pozdeyev Vitaly/Shutterstock Images
15: © Vladimir Arndt/Shutterstock Images
17: Goddard/SDO/GSFC/NASA
18: SDO/GSFC/JPL/NASA
20: © Tumeggy/Science Source
25: Goddard/GSFC/NASA
27: Goddard/GSFC/NASA
29: © Mopic/Shutterstock Images
33: © Detlev van Ravenswaay/Science Source
35: © Chris Butler/Science Source
37: © Paolo Gallo/Shutterstock Images
38: © Zhuravlev Andrey/Shutterstock Images
41: © Lukasz Janyst/Shutterstock Images
45: © Kit Leong/Shutterstock Images
49: NSF/AURA/NSO
51: KSC/NASA
53: JAXA/NASA/Flickr
55: Glenn Benson/KSC/NASA
56: © Buradaki/Shutterstock Images

ABOUT THE AUTHOR

Philip Wolny is an editor, author, and copy editor who was born in Bydgoszcz, Poland, and raised in Queens, New York. He currently resides in Florida with his wife and daughter.